The GOLDFISH *in the* Chandelier

Casie Kesterson   ❧   Illustrations by Gary Hovland

The J. Paul Getty Museum, Los Angeles

One week, a long time ago, I, Louis Alexandre, went to visit my great uncle, Henri.

Uncle Henri is old—even older than my mother and father. He lives in a house outside of Paris that was built by his grandfather Georges. And even though he is very old, Uncle Henri is very entertaining.

Uncle Henri is what my mother calls "dramatic," which makes him a good storyteller, and every time I visit, he tells me a new story about Alexander the Great, or *"Alexandre le Grand,"* which Uncle Henri always says while pretending to hold a spear in his right hand. My uncle says I have a lot in common with the famous Macedonian hero, and he calls me Louis Alexandre le Grand. This is because:

I am brave.

I am an expert general and loyal to my toy soldiers.

I am very imaginative.

You will hear a story about Alexander the Great later, but first I need to tell you a few other things.

In Uncle Henri's house, the bedrooms are on the top floor. Downstairs are the kitchen, the dining room, and the salon where my uncle likes to entertain us with stories and music. Uncle Henri's office is also downstairs, and that was the first place I went.

Uncle Henri was sitting at his desk, and it sounded like he was crying.

"What's wrong?"

"Oh, Louis," he said. "*Everything* is wrong!" He wiped an imaginary tear from his cheek. "I must design a chandelier for Madame Marie's salon. I have been designing chandeliers for over thirty years, and now my mind fails me! Boo hoo hoo hoo . . . aah hoo hoo hoo!" He buried his face in his hands.

I should tell you that my family has been making chandeliers for a very long time, and our workshop is full of them. So I was confident that I could solve his problem. "Don't worry, Uncle Henri," I said, patting his arm. "I'll help you."

My uncle sat up suddenly. "Will you?" he asked. "Will you, really?"

I picked up his pen and pulled his sketchbook toward me. I drew two U's, one above the other, and then a straight line right through them. When I finished, I pushed the sketchbook over to my uncle and smiled proudly.

My uncle studied the drawing and sighed. "Oh, Louis, if only it were that easy. Your chandelier is a perfectly good chandelier. It would certainly light the room. But Madame Marie's salon is dedicated to the four elements—Earth, Wind, Fire, and Water. And so I must design a chandelier that lights the room and incorporates all four elements. And it must be the most beautiful chandelier that Madame Marie has ever seen!"

Hmmm . . . Not as easy as I thought. But I am Louis Alexandre le Grand, and nothing is impossible!

The next day, after breakfast, I went to my uncle's office, and this
time I came prepared. I brought a crayon and paper, and several of my
soldiers, including the captain and the lieutenant, as reinforcements.

My uncle was lying on the floor, staring up at the ceiling.

"Hello, Uncle. I've come to help you with your chandelier."

Uncle Henri looked up at me. "Oh, thank goodness you're here.
Come and lie down on the floor with me. It will help us think."

"There is no better way to think up a chandelier than to first stare
at the ceiling!

Imagine Madame Marie's ceiling, and then the design for the chandelier will come to us," said Uncle Henri.

We lay there silently for a few minutes.

"Now, Louis, we mustn't rush this. Something will come to us."

We lay there for a few more minutes.

"I know it will come. It will just take time," said my uncle. "First, I think we need inspiration. How about a story?"

My uncle sat up. "Louis, as you know, there are many stories concerning the conquests of Alexander the Great." He paused and closed his eyes for a moment. "This is one of my favorites.

"One day," said Uncle Henri, "Alexander and his army reached the top of a giant mountain. Alexander felt so close to the sky that he decided he wanted to go up and see the heavens. He ordered his soldiers to build an invention, shaped like a large basket.

"Now, it happened," continued my uncle, "that on this mountain there lived griffins. So Alexander commanded his soldiers to capture some of the wild beasts and starve them for a few days."

"Oh, no! Hungry griffins!" I cried and took cover under my uncle's desk.

"When Alexander was ready to take flight, his men fastened the griffins to the large basket. Alexander climbed in, and his men handed him two long spears skewered with fresh pieces of liver. He held them out in front of the griffins, and they flew upward immediately, carrying Alexander up into the air.

"He soared through the clouds and could hardly believe all that was visible from the heavens—all of the stars and the great earth, far below him."

"Ho! Ho!" I said.

"And when he was satisfied that he had seen all that there was to see, he lowered the spears, and the griffins transported him back down to earth, to his army of men.

"And that is the story of Alexander the Great's flight. And now, my dear Louis, after all this talk of food, I am famished! May I interest you in a macaron or four?"

We went out onto the terrace. "You know, Louis," my uncle said, with a mouth full of macaron, "I have been thinking about your sketch of the chandelier, and that sketch is a good place for us to start. But it needs something more....Some chandeliers are decorated with leaves. What sort of decoration should we add to ours?"

"Soldiers!"

"Soldiers?"

"Yes, soldiers! To protect Madame Marie."

"That is a very good idea, Louis. A chandelier that lights the room AND protects Madame Marie! But remember, Louis, it must fit in with the scheme of the four elements: Earth. Wind. Fire. Water."

"Oh."

"But you've given me a thought. Alexander was a soldier, and when he was in the sky he saw the stars around him and earth below, correct?"

"Yes! Yes! The stars and earth!" I said, pretending to survey them, as if I were Alexander.

"Now, if I could only remember how he got up there. . . ."

"Griffins!"

"Griffins? Griffins, you say?"

"Yes! Yes!" I leaped up and started to run around in a circle, flapping my arms.

"Well, they do fly, don't they? And I suppose they need wind to do that, don't they?"

"Yes! Yes! Wind! Look, right there! We have the earth and the wind!"

"Oh, goodness, you're right, Louis! And our chandelier has branches that hold candles, correct?"

"Yes?!"

"Now if I could only remember what it is that I light those candles *with*. . . ."

"Fire! Fire!"

"Fire? FIRE? Oh, Louis, we have to get out of here!" Uncle Henri jumped to his feet.

"No! No! There is no fire here. Fire lights the candles!"

"Oh, yes, of course!" said Uncle Henri.

"Ahem!" Uncle Henri and I turned and saw my mother, standing in the doorway.

"Louis, it's time for your lesson."

"But we are designing a chandelier!" I cried.

My mother did not look convinced.

"Oh, all right." And I followed her inside for a lesson with my tutor, Monsieur Bernard.

Later that afternoon, I found Uncle Henri in his office, lying on the floor, once again.

"I am starting to see the chandelier now."

I lay down next to him. "Me, too."

A few minutes passed.

"But I don't see the whole chandelier," my uncle said.

"Me neither."

Maybe we need a story, I thought. And then I remembered. I sat up immediately. "I know: I can tell YOU a story."

"Oh, I *love* stories," said Uncle Henri. "Tell me! Tell me!"

"Do you know about the hot air balloon?" I asked. "The flight of the Montgolfier brothers?"

"I don't believe I do. Why don't you tell me?"

"When Monsieur Bernard was lecturing about the stars, I told him that I would like to see them up close. I said I could travel in a basket drawn by griffins, just like Alexander, up into the sky. Monsieur Bernard laughed. But then he asked if I knew that men had already traveled in the air *without* griffins. In the 1780s. They used a giant balloon." I made a big circle with my hands.

"Oh?" asked Uncle Henri. "Could this be true?"

"Yes. The idea came from two brothers, Joseph and Étienne Montgolfier. They made many tries with just the balloon, and finally, when it was ready, they sent up a duck, and a rooster, and a sheep, and—"

"No!" said Uncle Henri.

"Yes!" I replied. "And they were at VERSAILLES. In front of THE KING!"

"I can't believe it!" said Uncle Henri, shaking his head.

"Oh, Louis, that was a terrific story! Wouldn't it be nice if we could somehow incorporate the air balloon into our design?"

"Yes!"

"If only I could remember how it floated up. . . . "

"The fire. It heated the air inside the balloon, and the balloon went up."

"And do you suppose there was wind? Wind that caused it to be carried up and over the king, and up and over Paris?"

"Well, of course!"

We both lay back down and stared at the ceiling. "I think the chandelier is coming together," said Uncle Henri.

"Me, too," I said.

That night my father arrived from Paris. He had been working nonstop on the candlesticks and wall lights for Madame Marie's salon, and he wanted to talk to my uncle.

In the morning, my uncle and father were still talking, so I went out to the garden. There are lots of trees and bushes and flowers, and there are plenty of places to hide and stake out the enemy. Several gigantic trees. Many dense bushes. And some large rocks.

But the best thing about the garden is the pond. You can't see the bottom of the pond, but I will tell you in confidence that there is a hole at the bottom where the enemy can enter. Luckily, there are fish, so I charge them to guard the entrance.

I sat at the edge.

"There you are!" It was Uncle Henri.

"Shhh," I said quietly, pointing to the water. "We're on the lookout for the enemy."

"Oh, right!" said my uncle, in a near whisper.

"Do you suppose the fish are hungry after all of their hard work? Shall we feed them?" He held up a small loaf of bread.

I nodded.

Uncle Henri sat down next to me. He tore off a small piece of bread and gave it to me. I held it just at the surface of the water, and one of the fish came and took a bite.

"When I fly up into the air in the balloon with the griffins, I will want to take some fish with me as reinforcements."

"You are absolutely right, Louis," replied my uncle. "A good general is always prepared. Wait right here." My uncle rose, went into the house, and returned with a glass bowl. Quickly he dipped the bowl into the pond and scooped up water and two small fish.

"How's this?" asked Uncle Henri, handing me the bowl.

"Perfect!"

I lay down on the grass and carefully held the bowl above me to see how the fish looked up in the air. Uncle Henri stretched out next to me and we watched the fish swim around in the bowl above us.

"Wouldn't it be nice if we could incorporate the fish into our design, Uncle Henri?"

"Earth. Wind. Fire. Fish. Wait a minute – that doesn't sound right. What are the four elements again, Louis?"

"Earth. Wind. Fire. WATER."

"Oh, that's right. WATER. But we can't really *see* the water, can we?"

"No," I said, looking closely at the bowl. "Only the fish swimming."

And then it came to me. "But the fish can help us *see* the water. Like the griffins and the air balloon help us see the wind."

My uncle looked at me and smiled. "Brilliant, Louis!"

Over the next several weeks, back in Paris my father and uncle worked very hard, putting all the parts of the chandelier together, and the candlesticks and wall lights, too.

When the chandelier was completed, my mother, father,
Uncle Henri, and I made a visit to our workshop.
As soon as I walked through the door I saw the chandelier.

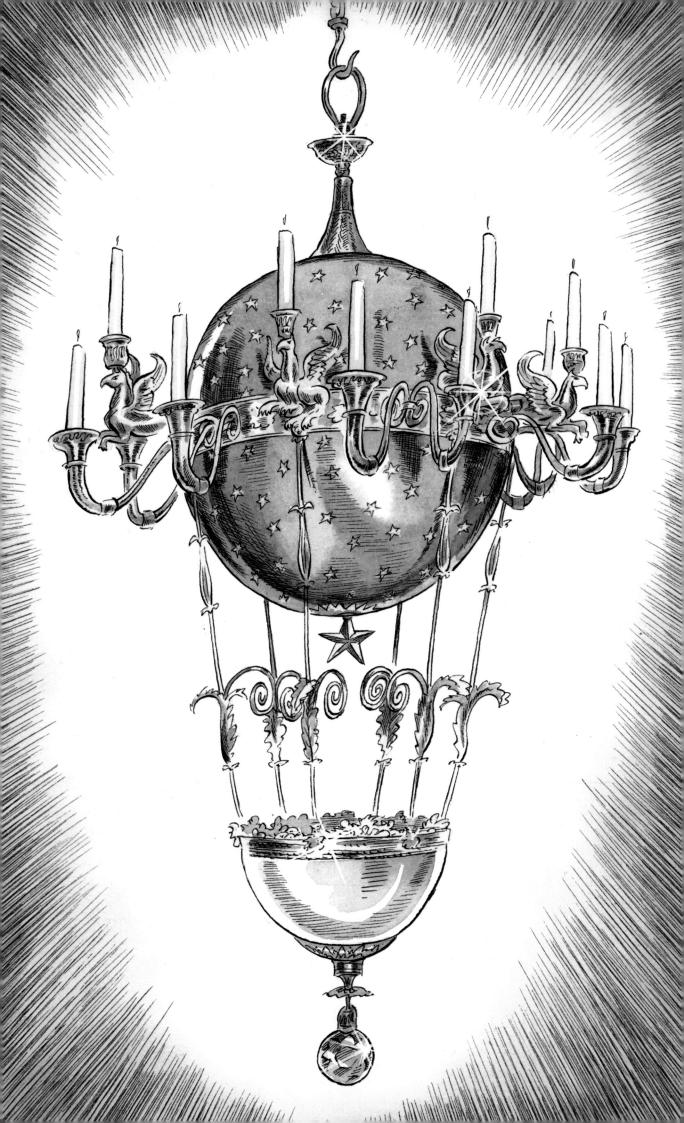

"Uncle Henri!" I said. "It is exactly as I imagined!"

"Me, too!" Uncle Henri replied.

"Louis," said my father, "tell us how the chandelier is ideal for Madame Marie's Salon of the Four Elements?"

I pointed to the blue sphere. "This is like the giant balloon made by the Montgolfier brothers years and years ago, back when Uncle Henri was a boy."

My uncle grimaced. "Really, Louis. It wasn't *that* many years ago."

I continued. "But the sphere is also round, like the earth. And it is covered in stars, so it looks like the earth and the starry sky at once. Just like what Alexander the Great saw when he went up in the air. And this is the basket that carried him," I said, pointing to a crystal bowl which hung below.

"Captivating, Louis!" said my mother. "Please, go on!"

"Here are the griffins," I said, pointing to the small monsters. "They hold the candles, and they help carry the giant balloon into the sky, like they helped Alexander."

"So the earth?" asked my father.

"The earth is the big, round sphere," I said.

"And the wind?" asked my mother.

"The wind carries the giant balloon high into the air and helps the griffins fly," I replied.

"And the fire?" asked my mother.

"The candles serve as fire. And they also help light the room."

"But what about the fourth element?" asked my father.

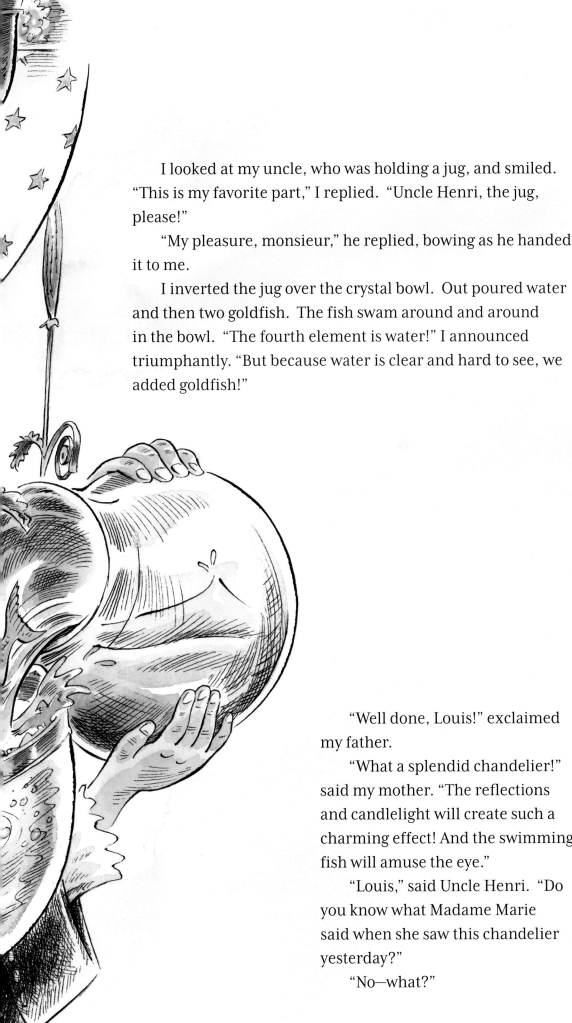

I looked at my uncle, who was holding a jug, and smiled. "This is my favorite part," I replied. "Uncle Henri, the jug, please!"

"My pleasure, monsieur," he replied, bowing as he handed it to me.

I inverted the jug over the crystal bowl. Out poured water and then two goldfish. The fish swam around and around in the bowl. "The fourth element is water!" I announced triumphantly. "But because water is clear and hard to see, we added goldfish!"

"Well done, Louis!" exclaimed my father.

"What a splendid chandelier!" said my mother. "The reflections and candlelight will create such a charming effect! And the swimming fish will amuse the eye."

"Louis," said Uncle Henri. "Do you know what Madame Marie said when she saw this chandelier yesterday?"

"No—what?"

Speaking like a very old woman, he replied: "'Monsieur Henri, this is the most beautiful chandelier. Alexander the Great himself would agree!'"

So that is the story of my chandelier. Probably when I grow up I will make more chandeliers, just like Uncle Henri.

But this will always be my favorite.

A Note from the Author

I hope you liked my story about this most spectacular chandelier in the collection of the J. Paul Getty Museum in Los Angeles. Although the chandelier does exist, many parts of the story are an invention of my imagination. Now, do you, the reader, have any questions?

Was the chandelier really made by Louis Alexandre and his uncle Henri?

Well. . .no. Louis Alexandre, Uncle Henri, and the rest of the characters are fictional, although they are like some of the people you'd find in Paris in the early nineteenth century.

The chandelier was made by Gérard-Jean Galle, who lived from 1788 to 1846. Galle, like his father Claude (1759–1815), was a bronze caster and gilder who lived and worked in Paris. Their workshop was well known for making all sorts of objects, such as clocks and wall lights, in addition to chandeliers.

Are casting and gilding bronze dangerous?

Very. They involve molten bronze and poisonous fumes.

Are there really griffins up there in the chandelier?

Yes, six griffins, in fact. And if you look closely, you will find some other creatures up there, too.

How old is the chandelier?

It was made about 1818–19.

Has it been at the museum all this time?

Not quite that long. The chandelier was acquired by the museum's founder, J. Paul Getty, in 1973.

Is this chandelier one-of-a-kind?

No, two other examples are known. One is in the Swedish Royal Collection in Stockholm. The second is in a private collection in the United States.

Did Alexander the Great really fly up into the heavens?

No, although Alexander the Great really was a famous Macedonian hero who lived a very long time ago—356 to 323 BC, to be exact. And because he was a legend during his lifetime, many incredible stories circulated about him.

Did the Montgolfier flight over Versailles really happen?

Yes. The flight with the animals took place on September 19, 1783, and the manned flight took place a few months later. And yes, the animals and the men landed safely.

What are macarons?

Small, round cakes made of almonds, sugar, and egg whites, which you eat like cookies. They are delicious. I am going to go have some now.

Do you have more questions? Get the answers and more at www.goldfishchandelier.com

Text © 2012 Casie Kesterson

Illustrations © 2012 Gary Hovland

© 2012 J. Paul Getty Trust
Published by the J. Paul Getty Museum, Los Angeles
Getty Publications
1200 Getty Center Drive, Suite 500
Los Angeles, California 90049-1682

John Harris, Editor
Kurt Hauser, Designer
Elizabeth Zozom, Production Coordinator

Printed and bound by Tien Wah Press, Singapore (W23223)
First printing by the J. Paul Getty Museum (12241)

Library of Congress Cataloging-in-Publication Data

Kesterson, Casie.
  The goldfish in the chandelier / Casie Kesterson ; illustrations by Gary Hovland.
    p. cm.
  Summary: In early nineteenth-century Paris, young Louis Alexandre helps his dramatic great-uncle
Henri design a spectacular chandelier for Madame Marie's salon. Includes author's note about a chandelier
in the J. Paul Getty Museum collection.
    ISBN 978-1-60606-094-0 (hardcover)
    [1. Chandeliers—Fiction. 2. Great-uncles—Fiction. 3. Paris (France)—History—1815–1870—Fiction. 4.
France—History—1815–1870—Fiction.] I. Hovland, Gary, ill. II. Title.
    PZ7.K4849Go 2012
    [Fic]—dc23
                            2011012961

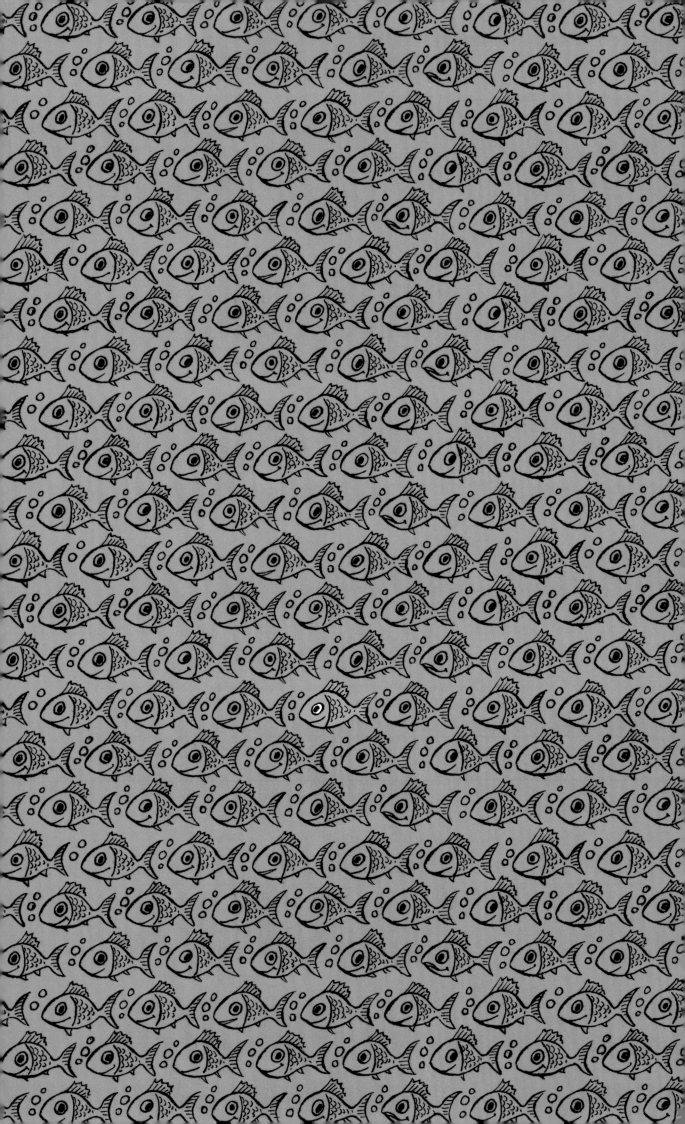